First published 2018, updated 2020

Paperback ISBN: 978-1976981456

About this Book

This book is designed to introduce children to the Italian language. Basic phrases are weaved together to form a story and to introduce the reader to the character.

Every double page displays the text in English and Italian, allowing the child to follow the story and learn both languages.

This book can be used as an early reader, or as a pre-school text.

Rachael & Rachele

A story in English and Italian by

AC Brown

Hello! My name is Rachael.

Ciao! Mi chiamo Rachele.

I am four years old.

Ho quattro anni.

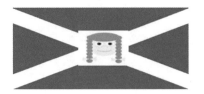

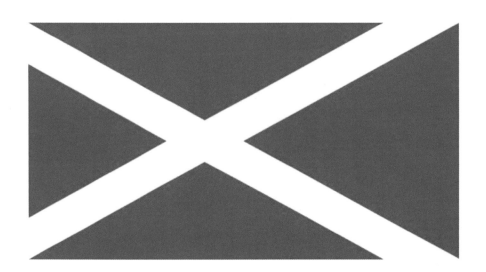

I live in Scotland.

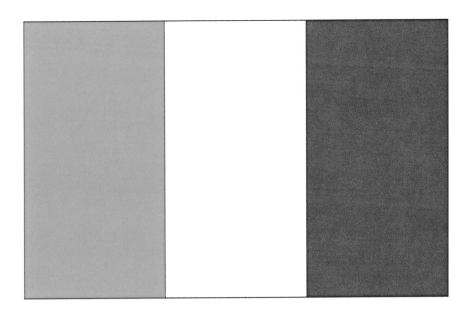

Habito in Italia.

I have a big brother called Thomas.

Ho un fratello maggiore di
nome Tommasso.

My favourite colour is yellow.

Il mio colore preferito è il giallo.

blue

green

red

purple

I also like blue, green, red and purple.

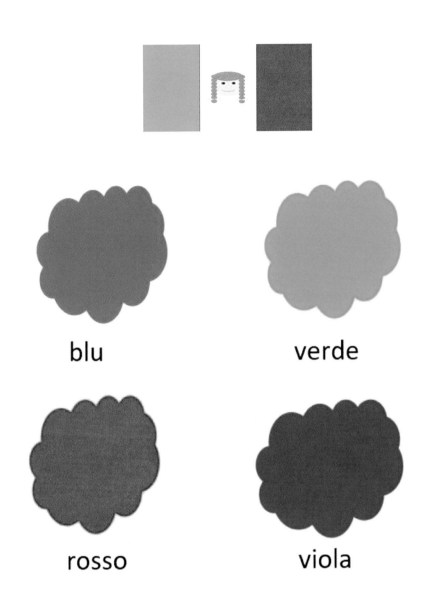

blu

verde

rosso

viola

Mi piacciono anche blu, verde,
rosso e viola.

I like riding my yellow bike.

Mi piace cavalcare la mia bici gialla.

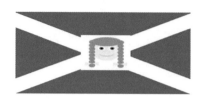

I enjoy playing tennis.

Mi piace giocare a tennis.

rain

sun

snow

I play outside in all weathers,
rain, sunshine and snow.

pioggia

sole

neve

Io gioco fuori in tutte le condizioni atmosferiche, pioggia, sole e neve.

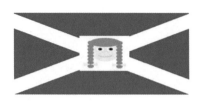

My best friend is a boy called Henry.

Il mio migliore amico è un ragazzo chiamato Enrico.

Sophie

Amira

Bethany

I also have friends called
Sophie, Amira and Bethany.

Sophie

Amira

Bethany

Ho anche amici che si
chiamano Sophie, Amira e
Bethany.

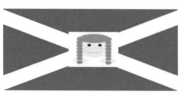

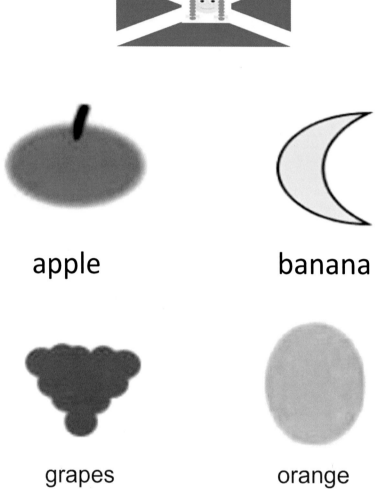

apple

banana

grapes

orange

I love fruit like apples,
bananas, grapes and oranges.

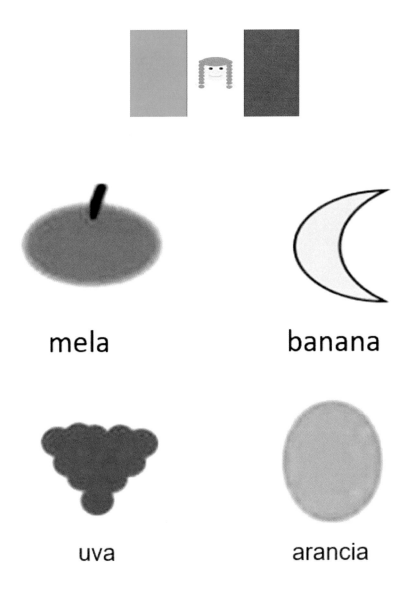

mela

banana

uva

arancia

Amo la frutta come mele, banane, uva e arance.

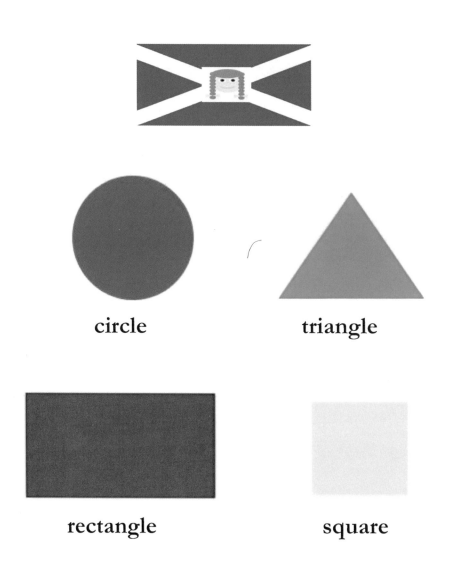

circle   triangle

rectangle   square

I enjoy drawing shapes like circles, triangles, rectangles and squares.

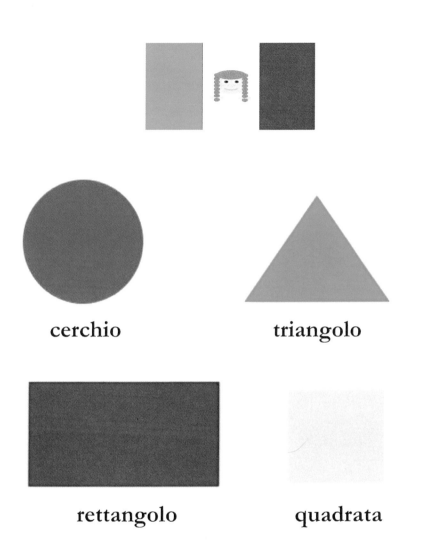

cerchio   triangolo

rettangolo   quadrata

Mi piace disegnare forme
come cerchi, triangoli,
rettangoli e quadrati.

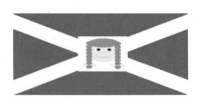

My bedtime is seven o'clock.

Le mia ora di andare a letto
sono le sette.

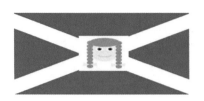

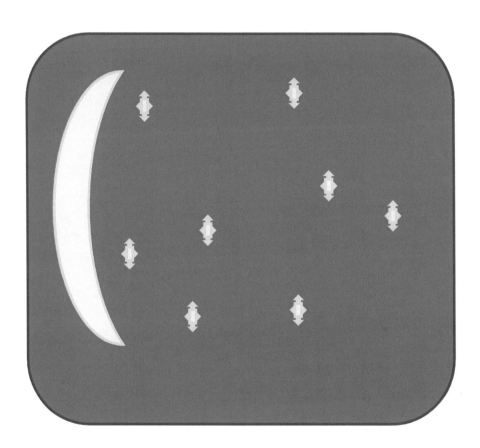

Goodnight!

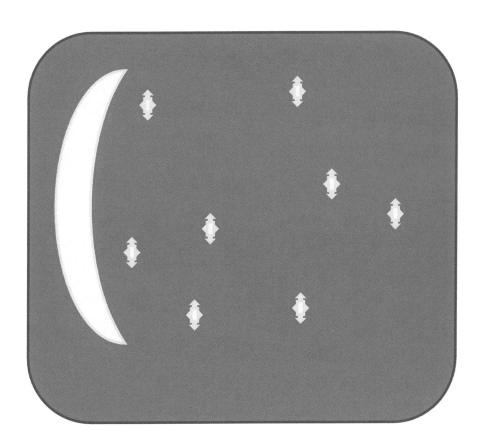

Buonanotte!

Made in the USA
Monee, IL
08 March 2023

29467292R00021